KRISTA'S
ESCAPE

GEMMA
JACKSON

POOLBEG

This book is a work of fiction. The names, characters, places, businesses, organisations and incidents portrayed in it are either the product of the author's imagination or are used fictitiously. Any resemblance to actual persons, living or dead, events or locales is entirely coincidental.

Published 2020
by Poolbeg Press Ltd.
123 Grange Hill, Baldoyle,
Dublin 13, Ireland
Email: poolbeg@poolbeg.com

A catalogue record for this book is available from the British Library.

ISBN 978178199-348-4

www.poolbeg.com

Also by Gemma Jackson

Through Streets Broad and Narrow

Ha'penny Chance

The Ha'penny Place

Ha'penny Schemes

Impossible Dream

Dare to Dream

Her Revolution

Published by Poolbeg

Foreword

DEAR READER,

Thank you for buying the first of my *Krista* novellas. I hope you enjoy the series. It's exciting for me to write these shorter stories so they can be delivered to you that much faster – as so many of you have requested.

I have a little office set up under my stairs. The only space in my small seaside home that was available. I sit and write about Krista and her life and I find myself marching up and down my hallway almost tearing my hair out. I shout aloud and plot. Did you know that after the war men were offered a college education and women were offered cookery classes so they could return to the kitchen? *Aaagh!* One of these days the men in the white coats are going to come for me. Do you think they will accept the fact that it is my writer's imagination making me act like a crazy person?

Krista is a new character for me. The first time we meet her she is 17 and unhappy at home. But the year is 1938 and we all know what is coming! WWII.

I am fascinated by the changes that the general public were forced to accept and learn to handle then. Young men and women had to leave the life they knew and any dreams they might have had, and step up to all that was demanded of them. Could you do it?

Now that the Official Secrets Act has expired and the wonderful women that served are allowed to speak of their service, I have read so many amazing true stories. I have laughed and cried as I read and found myself wondering what I would do if called upon to risk my life for my country. I am a bit old now but it doesn't take much imagination to put myself into the shoes of the women who served.

Because of my own love of the sea, I find that the books I choose to read are often about the WRNS – the Women's Royal Naval Service. Their daring and bravery leaves me breathless. I hope to share some of what I have learned with you without turning my books into a history lesson.

When we meet my main character Krista she is living in Metz, a little village on the French-German border.

Many, many years ago I attended a wedding in Metz. For those of you who don't know, a French wedding goes on for days. There is more than one ceremony. I think during that time I met every person in the village and was treated like royalty. I was the first foreigner to pass through there since the war! The villagers shared their war stories with me in little kitchens while producing amazing food. I sat in those kitchens stuffing my face and hearing stories that made the hair rise on my head. Little did I know that one day I would be able to use what I had learned.

Oh, what wonderful memories I have of Metz and the people I met there! My friend the bride was the only daughter, with eleven brothers. *Gasp*. Each one more handsome than the last. I was wined and dined and treated like a movie star.

I love to dance and have – well, had really, who knows where they are now – medals and cups for Latin and Ballroom dancing. The bride's brothers all danced. I was taken to the local café where the table and chairs were pushed back, the jukebox was turned on, and I was swept off my feet by those tall, dark, handsome men. The crowds cleared the floor and watched. I felt like Ginger Rogers and have never forgotten the wonder of the time I spent in what was a little out-of-the-way part of France.

So, come along with me on Krista's journey. I know I'll have fun writing it and hope you have fun reading it.

Gemma

Auberge du Village
Metz, France

Chapter 1

KRISTA DUMAS OPENED HER BLUE EYES at the first cheep from the birds greeting the coming dawn. She snuggled blissfully into her rough calico pillow. She loved this time of day when it felt as if she were the only human in the world awake.

This tiny room under the eaves was her place. The only part of the building where she could escape the demands of her family and the business they ran. It was time to start her day. She climbed carefully out of the narrow bed – she had hit her head off the wooden beams of the roof too many times to count. She took the few steps necessary to reach the rooftop window and, pushing upwards with her hands on the glass, she stood on her toes to put her head out of the opening.

She took a moment to appreciate the changing colours in the morning sky – all she could see from this vantage point.

She left her perch and walked over to the door with lowered head – the woollen dressing gown left behind by a visiting Englishman hung on one of the hooks on the back of the heavy wooden door. She pushed her arms into the sleeves before removing the chair from under the door handle and undoing the bolt. One could never be too careful while living in an auberge. She pulled open the door and on bare feet made her way to the wooden staircase leading down to the family rooms on the fourth floor. Practically holding her breath, she walked along the bare hallway towards the toilet.

She squatted over the Turkish toilet, smiling as always when she thought of the horror of some of their guests on first seeing the flat marble stand set into the floor of the guest toilets. She used the water hose set into the wall at the side of the toilet to flush – her mother objected to the rattle of pipes from a pulled chain. Having taken care of the rest of her business, she went back to her room to dress and start her day.

She glanced at the handsome leather-cased travelling clock standing on the ledge over her bed. It too had been left behind by a guest at the auberge. Krista had once suggested writing to the guests and informing them of their lost possessions. Her mother had slapped her around the ears at the very thought of the waste of time and the expense. If the guest was careless enough to leave items behind it was their hard luck in her mother's opinion.

Krista returned the chair to under the doorknob. She had to hurry. It was her duty to open the café-bar-tabac that her family ran from one side of the ground floor of the auberge. She had deliveries of breakfast breads to accept from the nearby boulangerie and there would be trouble if she did not have coffee brewing for the many early morning workers who stopped at the café each morning for coffee and a croissant.

She rushed around the room preparing herself to face the long day ahead. She took her black skirt and white blouse from the nail beaten into the wall. The outfit served as her uniform but it was also the only type of clothing she was allowed. Not for her the light bright clothing her age group wore. She pulled the hated black woollen stockings over her knees, then thick elastic garters to hold them in place. She'd carry her shoes down the stairs. She brushed her long white-blonde hair before forcing it into a heavy bun at the back of her neck with a sigh. She did wish her mother would allow her to adopt the short style so fashionable these days. The last thing she did before leaving the room was to take a long white apron that covered her from neck to hem from the back of the door. She checked herself as well as she could without a mirror before making her way silently down the long stretch of stairs to the ground floor.

"The excitement of my life!" Krista said aloud to herself. Why not? There was no one else around. "Coffee … where would we be without coffee?" she muttered as she prepared the machine for the day. "Can no one else clean this blessed machine? It is the same every

3

morning. I have to come downstairs a quarter of an hour early to clean the coffee machine. Could one of the men not do it when the place is closed at night? They could put the parts in to soak. Is that too much to ask?" She continued her grumbling as she soaked parts of the machine in boiling water.

Her movements were quick and familiar as she prepared the area for its first customers.

"I am not cleaning those windows." She knew she would. She couldn't bear to see smudges on the long windows that gave a view out onto the main street of their village. She pulled chairs off tables and set them on the floor. "At least the floor is clean. I suppose I should be grateful for that small mercy."

It saddened her to see a man she knew walk past without his usual wave and smile. How long had it been since anyone smiled to start their day? Now people stumbled along with heads down and shoulders hunched. "It is all so different," she whispered. Alone here she could admit to herself that she was scared. No one talked openly about the changes taking place in their world. The café-bar-tabac customers, who used to greet each day with loudly expressed opinions of everything under the sun, now huddled over their coffee and glanced under frowning brows at their neighbours. How long could such a state of affairs continue?

She was seventeen years old and sometimes felt as if she had the weight of the world on her shoulders.

"Maurice," she gasped when she opened the main doors to find a scowling young man and a visibly frightened youth standing on the other side. Her snippets of gossip that had at one time been the normal behaviour of this group. When had their world changed? Why was she noticing it so much this morning – was it because of Maurice?

She continued to work automatically. Part of her duty was to greet the auberge's early-rising guests when they left their rooms, and offer breakfast. The auberge had six large guest rooms on the second floor of the building. There was also shared accommodation offered on the third floor. The fourth floor and attics were the family's living quarters. She carried out her duties with a forced smile on her face, glad that her black skirt hid her trembling knees. She could not afford to break down. She served breakfast to their guests and local customers, took care of those wishing to check out and offered advice on walks and activities in the area to those who requested them.

The tour of the nearby Riesling vineyard that sat on the German side of the border was very popular with their guests. Baron von Furstenberg welcomed foreign visitors to his caves where his wines were sampled and sold in great quantities.

She desperately tried to pretend that all was as it should be, while at the back of her mind her thoughts buzzed like angry bees – had her father really promised her to Maurice La Flandre – surely not? She would never agree to such a union. They could not force her to accept him – could they? She had a throbbing headache long before the kitchen workers arrived. She prepared a tray of coffee to be carried up to her parents. She felt exhausted long before her mother came downstairs to take over the kitchen and begin overseeing the preparations for lunch.

Chapter 2

"*BONJOUR, JEAN-LUKE, HENRI, PHILIPPE.*"
Krista glanced at her three brothers when they entered
the café from the auberge stairway. They looked so
alike with their wide shoulders and slim hips, encased
in their uniform of white shirt and black trousers,
wearing highly polished black-leather shoes. They each
had black hair and brown eyes, much to the delight of
the ladies of the village. She tried to judge their mood
before she said anything more. They were bears in the
morning.

The three men grunted in response, strolling over to
take a table overlooking the main street of the village.
She poured three large thick white cups of coffee and
carried them over to the table.

"*Croissant*," Jean-Luke growled when she leaned over his shoulder to place the first cup of coffee in front of him – as the eldest he was always served first.

"*Pain au chocolat*." Henri took a packet of cigarettes from the breast pocket of his white shirt.

"How did you hurt your hands?" Philippe leaned forward to examine the bruises and nicks both of his brothers sported on their hands.

"Are you deaf? Get us something to eat!" Jean-Luke waved a dismissive hand towards Krista, ignoring his youngest brother's question

"There are no pastries left." Krista stood and waited for her brothers' abuse to break over her head. She stared down at them, refusing to cower. They all looked so alike while she, the only girl, was taller than all three and had white hair and blue eyes. A stranger would never believe they were related. She had always felt like the cuckoo in the nest of the Dumas family.

"*What?*" Jean-Luke pushed back his chair violently and stood to grab Krista's wrist. "What do you mean there are no pastries?" He shook her. "We have to be at work in the restaurant soon. *We* were working till early morning while you snoozed in your bed. The least we deserve is something to eat before we have to get to work!" He was angry with the world this morning. He hated this life of work and sleep for very little money. His parents claimed they were working for a better future for all of them. Well, as far as he was concerned, the future was now.

"Let her go, Jean-Luke, you are hurting her," Philippe said. "You are attracting attention." He pointed to the people walking past the long windows.

"Ah, you are useless!" Jean-Luke threw Krista's hand away from him, pushing her almost off her feet. "You have the easiest job of all of us. All you have to do is serve coffee and keep your eyes open while the rest of us sleep. Is even that too much to ask of you?" He pulled his chair close to the table and sat. "Now get us something to eat. It's almost time for us to open up. We need food to fuel us."

"We are here now, so you can run down to the boulangerie and get our order." Henri puffed on his cigarette, his eyelids half-mast because of the smoke.

"You don't think I thought about that already?" Krista hated the way her two eldest brothers looked at her. It made her flesh crawl. "I had young Hervé run down to the boulangerie when I saw we were running out of pastries. He said the shutters are closed and the Coutrille family are packing."

"*What?*" Philippe glared at his brothers.

"Yes, indeed, what?" Krista bent to glare at them. "What have you and your bully boys done to the Coutrille family?" She sniffed her disgust. "I had Maurice La Flandre in here this morning before the streets were aired. He was strutting and claiming his family had taken over the boulangerie. Would you know anything about that – *brothers?*"

"*Hold your tongue, girl!*" Henri viciously smashed his cigarette-butt into the big green ashtray on the table.

"Too many people are holding their tongues as far as I'm concerned!" Krista said.

Henri lit another cigarette and blew smoke in her face.

Krista glanced at the two men entering the café.

daughter a smile of greeting. She never did – all of her love and affection seemed to be reserved for her sons.

"No, Mama." What was the point in explaining about the boulangerie yet again? Her mother surely knew what was going on – her sons did not keep secrets from their mother. She would not allow it.

"Go to the kitchen and get something to eat. Then go to your room. I will have Hélène keep an eye on the café."

"But, Mama –"

"Do as I tell you." Emilie was not in the mood to take cheek from anyone. Those stupid sons of hers! Had they even given a thought to the business before they attacked the Coutrille family? No. It was that simple. They followed the crowd, never thinking for themselves. And where was Philippe when she needed him? Why had she been given such a burden? Then there was this great gawk of a girl staring at her out of injured blue eyes. What was to become of her? Emilie felt very hard done by and wished she could slap some sense into the men of her family. She hadn't time to do that. She had a business to run.

"Mama –"

"Krista, I have no time for theatrics – do as I tell you – get something to eat and go to your room." She smoothed the lush fabric of her dress with lily-white hands. "I will send for you when matters have been discussed. Now away with you!" She waved her hand towards the door leading from the café into the auberge.

"Yes, Mama."

Chapter 3

"GO TO YOUR ROOM LIKE A NAUGHTY infant!" Krista pulled open the wooden door to the outdoor laundry building with one hand while ripping at the straps that held her long apron in place with the other. She was angry and frightened – not a good mood to be in. "Well, I won't be sent to my room."

She closed the door to the laundry room behind her. There were enough cracks in the door and window fittings to allow plenty of air and natural light inside. No need for extra illumination. The long building was deserted. The laundry women would be taking lunch in the room behind the kitchen set aside to allow the staff to eat in privacy. She pushed her way carefully through the rows of damp white sheets hanging from the ceiling, waiting to be ironed.

The crackle and rattle of money in her apron pocket startled her. Goodness, she thought, in all of the fuss I forgot to leave the morning takings with Mama. She will be furious. The takings were low this morning. I suppose I'll get blamed for that too. Still, I did sell several crates of the house wine. That should be good news for her.

The café-bar-tabac stocked wine for the villagers to purchase. They made good profit on the house wine and sales of that seemed to please her mama.

She removed the money from her apron along with the letter Philippe had given her. She laid everything out carefully on top of one of the closed straw baskets. The deep baskets with leather straps were shaped like chests and were carried around the auberge to distribute fresh laundry. When she was sure she'd removed everything from the pocket she threw the apron into one of the tall wide straw baskets sitting around the floor.

Her mother was adamant that they all keep their clothing clean. They should at all times be wearing one outfit, have one clean and one in the laundry. She seemed to chant that at least ninety times a day, or so it seemed to Krista. The demands for clean laundry for the auberge itself seemed to be never-ending. She was glad she wasn't the one who had to stand all day over boiling copper kettles.

She was about to shove the money and envelope into the pockets of the skirt she wore when she noticed her clean uniform hanging on a nail, ready for her to take to her room. Without thought she removed her uniform, confident she would not be disturbed – midday was after all sacred – people would be eating at this time. She wasn't hungry. She put the clothes she removed into the appropriate baskets and quickly dressed. She put the envelope from Philippe into one of the deep pockets of her fresh skirt, pinning them in place. The money she folded into a clean white handkerchief before putting it into her skirt pocket. She pushed one of the closed baskets towards the window that overlooked the street and dropped down onto it with a sigh. She needed to think. So much in her world was changing.

The auberge sat on a large corner lot. The café opened onto the main street and one of the side streets, rue d'Eglise, allowing easy flow for customers in both directions. The side street was convenient for deliveries. The laundry building overlooked the side street. Madame Dumas had threatened to have the window nailed shut whenever she found her staff hanging out of it, chatting with friends and neighbours. Krista was glad she hadn't. She pushed up the bottom of the sash window, thankful for the fresh air that blew inside.

She leaned against the whitewashed wall, out of sight of anyone who might be passing. She sucked in fresh air, closing her eyes briefly. She sometimes felt the auberge was a prison. She had been working in the family business since she could toddle. First fetching and carrying under the watchful eye of Grand-mère Dumas, a woman who had been sparing with praise but fast with a knuckle-jab. She had worked before school and after school for as long as she could remember. She was never allowed to run free as some of her classmates were.

She had no close friends. Only Hanna, who also worked in her family business, had ever really understood how frustrated she sometimes became. What would she do without Hanna to run to? She had lied to her brothers. She hadn't sent a young boy to check the boulangerie, she had run down herself. She had knocked and shouted at the door for Hanna but no-one answered. Where was her friend?

Footsteps crunched on the walkway outside the laundry building. Krista hoped whoever it was would visit one of the other outbuildings. She was enjoying this peaceful period.

"We will find what we need in here."

She recognised that voice. Her father. What was he doing here? He should be tending to business in the dining room. *Don't see me!* She closed her eyes and prayed. *Please, don't see me!*

"You are sure she is in her room?"

Krista could almost feel her blood freeze in her veins. Maurice La Flandre, what was he doing here? She was afraid to move. She willed them to remain near the entrance door. She was deep inside the building. The damp hanging sheets should hide her from their view. Unless they walked down the long building. She clenched her teeth and took slow deep breaths through her nose. Her heart was beating so hard she was afraid they would hear it.

"Of course she is in her room. Her mother gave her an order. She knows better than to disobey an order from her mother."

The striking of a match sounded. Papa never went anywhere without his cigarettes.

"You said the attic bedroom door has a bolt. I may have to kick it in." This was followed by a nasty male snigger.

"No, that won't be necessary. She only locks the door at night to protect her virtue." Papa Dumas coughed.

Krista could imagine him dropping the cigarette onto the ground and stamping it out with the heel of his shoe. How many times had she seen him do the exact same thing? Such a waste – he took one or two puffs then threw the cigarette away. Why was she thinking such rubbish?

"That won't be a problem after today." Maurice laughed. "*I'll* be taking her virtue." He sniggered. "Make no mistake, after today she will be mine."

"I promised you could have her, didn't I?"

Krista had to slap a hand over her mouth when a gasp of horror tried to escape. What kind of man was her father that he would offer her to one such as Maurice La Flandre? The whole village knew he was a bully and a brute.

"She will fight you," Papa Dumas warned with audible relish.

"That will please me greatly. I enjoy beating sense into stupid female heads."

"I'd like to help you. That is one female who considers herself higher than the rest of us. Here, grab one end of this. It's the reason I brought you out here. You had best take something with you to tie her up."

She heard the sound of tearing fabric. That explained

24

what they were doing here. They must be tearing up one of the old sheets kept for rags.

"Be sure to push something into her mouth or she'll scream the place down," Papa Dumas warned. "The wife will not be happy if her guests are disturbed."

The ripping of fabric sounded again.

"You are going to make an honest woman of her, aren't you?"

"I told you I would."

"And you will be sure to tell the Führer's men of my co-operation?"

"Of course, of course."

The loud blare of a claxon sounded on the street.

"Shit, we'd better get out of here before someone sees us together," Papa Dumas said.

The two men left the room, closing the door at their backs. Krista wanted to collapse onto the floor and wail her woes to the world. She couldn't. She didn't have time.

"*Hurry along, old thing!*" A crisp English voice broke the silence of the street and the bleeping of the car claxon sounded again. "I had a dashed difficult time finding this place. Rue d'Eglise, for heaven's sake – why can't the Frenchies call it Church Street and be done with it?"

Krista dropped to her knees to look out the window. A large stylish British car sat close to the curb outside the window. She knew it was English because the driver was sitting on the wrong side of the vehicle. She wondered who it belonged to. They had no English guests at the moment.

"Perhaps because this is their country and they speak French?"

Krista recognised that voice. It was Miss Andrews, the lady who rented a small cottage in the mews that ran along the back of the auberge. Krista had taken English lessons from her for many years. She was a gentle lady and Krista had always felt comfortable in her company.

"Don't be like that, old girl." The driver, a portly bald man in a tightfitting tweed suit, pushed his way out of the car. He stood by the open door, shouting without regard for anyone else. "I want to get on the road while the natives are having their three-hour lunch. We should have the road to ourselves. I had the little auberge here pack us a picnic. So do hurry along, old thing!"

"I need help carrying my luggage."

"I can't leave the car." The gentleman sounded highly indignant. "It took a dashed long time to crank her up. I am not turning the engine off. Is there not a lad around who would be glad to earn a few francs?"

"No, there is not – I need the assistance of your manly muscles," Miss Andrews snapped. "Leave the darn thing on – there would be more danger of it being stolen if it were a pushbike. How many people in this village do you think could drive that behemoth, and with the wheel on the opposite side?" She snorted through her nose, a noise Krista was very familiar with. "Now come along." She turned to go back to her little house.

"Oh, very well." The driver closed the door of the car gently and walked away without locking his vehicle. He disappeared down the laneway, following on Miss Andrews' heels.

Krista had no time to think. No time to plan. She must move now. She would rather find herself thrown out of that car onto the side of the road than in the clutches of Maurice La Flandre.

She pushed up the window, sticking her head out slowly to check the way was clear. She looked at the white blouse she wore and almost groaned. She needed something dark. She looked around and spotted a man's black suit jacket hanging on a hook behind the door. She didn't know who it belonged to, but her need was great. She shoved her arms into the sleeves and, with a final glance to be sure the coast was clear, crawled out of the window, almost falling headfirst into the street. She took time she could ill afford to close the window behind her. She wanted to leave no clues as to where she had gone.

She bunny-hopped over to the car and with desperate fingers and a prayer on her lips reached to open the back door. She almost threw her body into the space along the floor behind the front seats. She used the leather hoop to close the door behind her and, making herself as small as she could, aligned herself along the new-smelling carpet.

She did a frantic mental check of her person. For once in her life she could be grateful for the dark colour of the hated woollen stockings she was forced to wear. She pulled the strange-smelling jacket over her head and face, making sure it still covered her white bouse. She should be well hidden under the black fabric. Praying as she never had before in her life, she waited to see if she would be discovered.

"I still say you could have left a great deal of this rubbish behind you!"

The door at Krista's feet opened and something heavy was thrown on top of her legs. She bit her lip and fought to remain silent.

"*I refuse to listen to any more of your grumbling, old thing!*"

A bag, fortunately soft, was thrown on top of Krista's head and shoulders. They must be standing on either side of the car, shouting at each other. She thanked whatever fates were protecting her for their absorption in their argument.

"You are the most contrary of women," the man huffed.

"Just a few more items and then we can be on our way." Miss Andrews slammed the door at Krista's head.

"Steady on, old thing! There is no need to damage my vehicle!"

The door at her feet was closed gently.

She heard them get into the front of the car and slam the doors. Then the car moved off and it was impossible to hear if they said anything more over the deep growl of the engine. Was Miss Andrews going on a trip? Surely she would have heard? This was a small village and everyone knew everyone else's business. But it didn't matter. This sudden trip was a blessing for Krista. She wanted to move the bags to a more comfortable position but was afraid to move.

"Did you really have someone pack a picnic?"

These were the first words Krista heard from Miss Andrews since the car rolled out of the village.

They were on their way. She had done it. She had escaped.

"I am hungry," Miss Andrews said. "This sudden flight of yours caused me to miss lunch. Still, I suppose a free journey home is always welcome."

"*Hmm*. In answer to your question, I do have a picnic basket, but I didn't ask the auberge to pack it. Too many of the wrong sort of people in there."

"Oh really, Ger–"

"*Bertram!*" the driver snapped. "It's *Bertram* – remember it – *Bertram*."

"You're being ridiculous. We are in the car driving along deserted roads and still you insist on this fiction."

"Have you forgotten everything you learned in the last war, my dear?"

"I cannot believe we are coming to this again." Miss Andrew's voice broke slightly. "Two wars in one lifetime seems too much to bear." There was a moment of silence. "I wanted to hide away in my little mews cottage and ignore all of it."

"Nowhere will be safe with that madman in control."

"I still don't understand why you insisted I accompany you."

The sound of pinched leather carried to Krista. She imagined Miss Andrews must be twitching in her seat.

"And why do I have to wear this ridiculous hat? I only have the thing to allow the children I tutor to play dressing-up!"

"We need to have the appearance of an eccentric English couple exploring the country and staring at foreigners. As to why I insisted you accompany me, well, it is very simple, my dear. I need your contacts."

Chapter 4

KRISTA LAY ON THE CAR FLOOR, listening to her companions talk. She understood the words but had difficulty understanding the meaning of their conversation. She wondered where they were going and how soon she should make her presence known. She needed a plan. For the first time in her life she was on her own. She could plan for her own future only if she had any idea of what that future should, could or would be.

If the pair in the front seats were not too angry with her, they might agree to take her to the nearest train station. She had the morning takings from the café in her pocket. It wasn't a great deal of money but it would be enough to buy her a train ticket to Paris or

and, thinking perhaps Miss Andrews was the safer option, stepped out of the car on her side and into an area of wide-open countryside. There wasn't even a cow in sight. She didn't try to run. What was the point? They had the car and guns. With her hands in the air, she stepped away from the car.

"You ladies go into the bushes there." The driver waved his gun in their direction. "It will be primitive but after using those confounded Turkish toilets I doubt you will be offended."

"Miss Andrews –" Krista began.

"Hush, child." Miss Andrews didn't lower the handgun. "I will wait while you relieve yourself. I advise you not to run while I tend to my own business."

Krista meekly went ahead as they walked towards the bushes.

When they returned, the car doors were all closed and the driver had a tartan blanket spread over the grass. He had opened the large wicker picnic basket and spread the food out. Krista's stomach grumbled. It had been a long time since she'd eaten. The driver was holding a sheaf of papers in one hand and the look in his eyes caused Krista to trip over her own feet.

"What is the matter?" Miss Andrews asked as soon as she saw the expression on her travelling companion's face. "Oh, by the way, Bertram, I think you should know that Krista here was one of my best students. She speaks and understands English perfectly."

"I found this in the back of the car." He shook the man's black jacket. He pointed the gun at Krista, his finger steady on the trigger. "Who does it belong to?

The only reason you are still breathing is because it obviously belongs to a man. What man? What is his name? *Who does this belong to?*" He was shouting now, the veins in his neck standing out starkly.

"I don't know ... I swear I don't!" she cried when the gun was once more waved at her. "I found it in the laundry room at the auberge. I needed something to hide the white of my blouse."

"Why?"

"I saw your car from the laundry-room window. You were my only chance of escape. I had to have something to hide my white blouse or you would have seen me straight away. I swear that is all I know. The jacket was hanging on a hook behind the laundry-room door. I grabbed it just before I hid in your car. I swear it." Krista was shaking.

"What is it, Bertram?" Miss Andrews said from behind Krista's back.

"Orders, my dear," the man bit out. "Orders of the vilest kind."

"Let us all sit down," Miss Andrews said. "We present quite the tableau for any passing motorist to see." She walked around Krista's rigid body and knelt down elegantly on one side of the blanket on the grass. "Krista will not run. I give you my word." She put her handgun under the edge of the blanket. "Where would she go?"

"Very well." The man never took his eyes off Krista as he sat down on the blanket. He too put his gun under the edge of the blanket. "Sit down and you may explain to us how you ended up in the back of my car."

She didn't move.

"*Sit, sit!*" he ordered.

Krista joined them on the blanket. She was afraid to move while the other two unpacked the picnic basket. She stared at the items being removed. The bread, sausage and wine were all German not French. She tried not to show her surprise.

"What?" the man suddenly demanded. "What are you looking at? Tell me? Something has made you stare." He reached for the spot on the blanket that concealed his gun.

"The food is German!" Krista gasped, before he could once again threaten her with that evil weapon.

"It would appear, Bertram, my dear, that you have been out of the game for too long." Violet Andrews smirked. "Such a simple error could get us all killed."

"We will eat and drink the evidence of my failure while we listen to this young one's story." He poured wine into three of the four glasses he had removed from the lid of the picnic basket. "I want to know how she ended up in my car and then I will have some idea of what is to become of her. But only after she answers my questions about that jacket and who it might possibly belong to."

"That is sure to give anyone an appetite." Miss Andrews applied herself to the food. She was hungry and didn't particularly care where the food had come from.

"Well, young woman," he sipped his wine, staring over the glass at Krista, "begin."

"I don't know where or when to begin."

"The beginning is usually the best place," Miss Andrews said.

"Well, this day started off badly with Maurice La

Flandre coming into the café claiming his family were taking over the village boulangerie ..."

Krista paused as she leaned over to help herself to some German bread and sausage. It would make a nice change from the mainly French food served at the auberge.

The only sound for a long time was that of eating as they calmed their hunger and Krista's voice as she recounted the events of her day up to and including being discovered in the car. Violet Andrews noticed that Krista's appetite did not seem to be affected by her peril. Ah, what it was to be young!

"I can well believe that Dumas would try to save his own skin by offering Krista up to La Flandre," Violet commented to her companion when Krista had recounted her tale.

Krista was looking down at the blanket, now void of any foodstuff. She wanted to cross her fingers while she waited for the verdict to be passed on her story.

"Someone should have put a bullet in that young man's head long ago." The man pushed to his feet.

"Please," Krista was afraid to move without permission, "may I see that jacket? I grabbed it in haste, grateful to find something I could use to hide myself under. I didn't really look at it but it has been over my head since we left the auberge. There is a smell lingering in it that I can't place. Perhaps if I could look at the jacket I would know to whom it belongs."

"If I am not mistaken it smells of blood!" he barked.

"Maurice La Flandre, could it be his?" Krista could think of no-one else at the auberge who might have bloodstains on their jacket. Then she thought of her two eldest brothers. Hadn't Philippe questioned them about the grazes on their hands this morning?

"The young man's a fool – but surely even he would know better than to leave such evidence of his crimes lying about." He shook the papers he held in a white-knuckled fist.

"Maybe he was distracted," Krista whispered. "He seemed very eager to reach my room and inflict pain." She remembered the gasping quality of his voice as he spoke of beating her.

"We must bury this jacket. But these papers are important. We will hide them somewhere in the car or about our persons where they will not be found. Come along, hurry, we must be on our way."

He gestured for them to stand before pulling the blanket from the grass, shaking it and throwing it into the rear of the car.

"But what about me?" Krista stood staring at her two companions with her mouth open. They were in the middle of nowhere. Were they just going to leave her?

Chapter 5

THE DRIVER'S EYES TRAVELLED OVER Krista from head to ankles. He stood for a moment with his hands on his hips, looking around the remote area he had chosen for their first stop. He sighed deeply and turned his attention back to the women.

"Violet," he said, "can you make this," one hand made a sweeping gesture over Krista's figure, "young woman look less like our dinner waitress and more like our travelling companion?"

"I'll try, but ..."

"Just do it." The driver turned back to the car. "I have a shovel in the car. I'll bury this jacket while you sort her out."

"*Wait!*" Krista held out a hand as if to touch the

German regime." Krista's heart broke as she read aloud the names of her neighbours – people who had never hurt anyone in their lives.

"The horror!" Miss Andrews dropped her face into her hands while her shoulders shook.

They motored through the village until they were once more in remote countryside.

Silence reigned as they travelled the miles towards the port of Antwerp. The three passengers were lost in their own thoughts. They looked at the pretty countryside and villages they passed through but didn't really see them.

"We are nearing the Flemish town of Mecelen," the driver said that evening, his voice startling the two women who were dozing with their heads leaning against the car widows.

"Thank heavens," Miss Andrews said over a yawn.

They had stopped earlier in the day at one of the many villages they passed through. Krista had been tasked to refill the empty picnic basket and a flask. They had eaten in the car, stopping only to take care of their bodily needs at the side of the road.

Chapter 6

"NOW, YOUNG LADY ..." THE DRIVER pinned Krista in place with the force of his glare.

They had arrived in Mercelen and rented a suite of rooms in one of the many hotels around the village square. The suite was made up of two large bedrooms and a sitting room.

Krista was almost asleep standing upright. She wanted only to lie down in one of the rooms and stretch the aches from her body, but it didn't appear she would get to retire yet.

"I have seen you studying me. You appear to know who I am ..." The driver's voice jerked Krista's attention back to him. "How?"

Miss Andrews was sitting by the side of a glowing

fire – a silent witness.

"Herr Baron –" Krista was too tired to even think of lying, "you have shaved off all your hair. You have made yourself bald, done away with your beard and moustache but I can still see you."

"What about my figure?" He held out his arms to display his body, still clothed in the unattractive tweed suit.

"I do not know what you have done to appear portly but you stride with confidence around the place and your hands … well, Herr Baron … they are not the bloated hands of a portly individual." She had stared at those hands as they held a loaded pistol pointed at her.

"Out of the mouths of babes," Miss Andrews said softly.

"Go to bed." He pointed to one of the bedrooms. "You will share that room with Miss Andrews. Go, you are almost asleep already."

"Yes, sir." She bit back the comment that trembled on her lips. He would be almost asleep too if he'd had to rise as early as she had.

She walked towards the bedroom door, wondering what she would sleep in. She had only the clothes she stood up in.

"The maid has unpacked for me," Miss Andrews said. "You may choose something of mine to sleep in."

"Thank you, Miss Andrews," Krista said over her shoulder.

She entered a bedroom well-lit by the gas lamps the maid had left burning. The large double bed looked very inviting. She was so tired she was almost stumbling. She selected a nightgown from Miss Andrews' possessions stored in the chest of drawers. With a yawn wide enough to break her jaw she began to undress to the skin. She would have to wear these clothes again tomorrow. She shoved her hands into the pockets of her skirt, something she did habitually, and discovered the handkerchief-wrapped money and the letter from her brother. So much had happened today that she had forgotten all about them.

She removed the items and put them on top of the chest of drawers. She pulled on the nightdress and, with a tired sigh, hung her outer clothing on one of the satin-wrapped hangers in the large wardrobe.

Wearing the borrowed nightdress, she dropped onto the side of the bed to read the letter from Philippe.

Kris,

I do not have much time but you must know. You are not my blood sister. You are no relation to me or mine. I do not say this to hurt you but feel you should know. We are not of the same blood. I don't know where you come from and only know this much from conversations overheard between my parents.

Kris, somehow the auberge belongs to you. I am not sure how but the auberge is part of the price paid to my parents to raise you as their own.

I am sorry to tell you in this fashion but I could not leave without telling you at least this much.

That is all I have time for. I am leaving. I will

not be a part of whatever is happening at the auberge.

Take care of yourself. These are dangerous times.

With affection,
Philippe
PS. I will always consider myself your big brother.

Krista fell back onto the bed, the letter in her hand. What was she to think of that? She was no relation of the Dumas family. She turned her head into the pillow, trying to make sense of what she had just learned. She was not related to the people she had always thought of as her family.

Thank God.

She fell asleep on top of the covers, the letter still clutched in her hand.

"What are we to do with our little stowaway?" Violet Andrews asked.

The two were seated at a table pulled close to the window, overlooking the town square. They had ordered room service. They had enjoyed their meal and were sitting enjoying coffee and cognac while watching the world go by.

"We will have to take her with us." Gerhardt von Furstenberg ran a hand over his bald pate. It was strange to be without hair but he'd been willing to make the sacrifice. He knew his days were numbered. It was only a matter of time before they came for him as they had for so many of his friends. Even so, the young girl had seen through his disguise. He would have to be more careful – more lives than his depended on him escaping.

"We certainly cannot leave her to the tender mercies of La Flandre." Violet was incensed. "How could Dumas offer her to that ignorant bully?"

"Calm yourself, my dear. It did not happen."

"Only through the merest chance. How on earth did you ever believe that leaving her with the Dumas family was a good idea?"

"What was I to do?" Gerhardt picked up his glass of cognac, grabbed the bottle from the table in his free hand and gestured towards the fire. "Come, let us sit in more comfort."

"You surely could have found a more caring family." Violet followed him to the fireplace, not willing to let the subject drop. She had wondered for years how the situation with the Dumas and Krista had come about.

"Lord, all of that seems so long ago, yet sometimes it feels like only yesterday." Gerhardt put the cognac bottle on the floor by his armchair and sat back with a sigh, He looked into the amber depths of his glass, swirling the liquid around as he remembered. "My poor brother, to have survived the war and then to be killed so tragically. If it had been anyone else I would have laughed – killed by a cow." He shook his head and fought the pain the memory of his brother brought. His brother and his lover died when he crashed his car into a cow on a country lane in the dark.

"Constance died too." Violet sipped her cognac.

She, Constance and their friends in the Women's

Royal Naval Service had come through so much mayhem and madness together. Constance's death at that time and in such a way seemed doubly tragic. Violet had been in England at the time, one of many women desperately trying to keep the Women's Royal Naval Service afloat. The dedicated women of the WRNS under the skilled leadership of Dame Katharine Furse had formed an efficient, tightknit, formidable force during WWI. When war ended the shock of being patted on the head, thanked for their contribution and sent back to the kitchen had left them all reeling. It had been a horrible time. Constance had agreed to serve as secretary to a member of the British foreign office. She had been in Berlin during the difficult years of returning peace to Europe.

"Yes, indeed, it was a miracle the babe survived." The placement of a small baby had been the least of his worries at that time. His brother's death had changed his world. He had been forced to accept the responsibility of the schloss, its estates and its people. He was never meant to be Baron von Furstenberg. His brother had filled that role admirably until he met Constance Grace. The actions of the pair of lovers were still sending ripples out into the world.

"So, the Dumas." Violet wasn't going to give up now that she had him talking. She had never felt free to question him before.

"It was a desperately difficult time, Violet," Gerhardt said. "I had lost a much-loved older brother. A brother who had abandoned all of his responsibilities for love." He bit it out through his teeth. "I was placed in a position that taxed my every nerve. I had my brother's widow and young daughters to consider. My brother had been the heir. The Golden Boy. I was the spare and I enjoyed that position. I never wanted to be Baron von Furstenberg."

"You have made a darn fine fist of it from what I have seen and heard." Violet had never really considered the effect of that terrible accident on this man.

"Thank you." Gerhardt bowed his head slightly in her direction. "I felt, for many years, that I was running in place."

The estate and indeed the world had been trying to recover from a world war. The estate and its people had been hanging on to their way of life by the skin of their teeth. Every decision he'd had to make seemed of world-shaking importance at that time. Now, the moment he felt as if he could relax and enjoy the way of life he'd struggled to create, whispers of war rose up again.

"You had your wife and sons to consider too." Violet wondered how much support this man had received.

"I left the running of the schloss and the family to my wife. I had to concentrate on the vineyard and our investments. There were a great many mouths to feed." That had been a mistake but he was only one man. He could not be everywhere and do everything. "My brother and I married in haste at the outbreak of war. It was, perhaps, not the best decision either of us ever made." He would not disparage his wife. He had made vows to the woman. He'd been shocked by her almost obscene glee at becoming Baroness – her eldest son was now the heir. She lorded it over everyone in a most unattractive fashion.

"Your wife would not accept the care of your brother's child?" Violet wondered how she would feel in the same situation – but surely there were nannies at the schloss?

"I did not ask." Gerhardt shuddered at the very thought. His family would have destroyed the poor thing.

"So, the Dumas family?"

"It seemed by far the best idea at the time. They were struggling to pay the lease on the auberge. The war had been difficult for everyone." He sighed deeply. "The wife had just lost a babe and was having a hard time recovering, according to Monsieur Dumas." He looked across the fire at his companion. "She had the milk the baby needed. What was I to do?"

"If I had known in time, I might well have taken the baby myself," Violet said.

"You were still fighting passionately trying to keep the WRNS together." Gerhardt knew of this only because his brother had shared his admiration of these women and his lover Constance with him. "Even had I known of your existence I would never have asked you to drop everything to run to my aid."

"Fat lot of good our efforts and determination did for anyone." Violet didn't like to think of the desperate times after the war when the ministry disbanded the WRNS. They had begged to be allowed to remain the tightknit force they had been. They had offered to work for nothing. All to no avail. They were no longer needed. Thrown away – discarded.

"They will need the WRNS again now," Gerhardt said. "Have you thought of that?"

"It has been so long … too long perhaps. We kept in touch after we were disbanded but so many of the girls went on to do other things." They had formed many associations to keep the spirit of the Wrens, as they were popularly known, alive. She still received her copy of the monthly magazine *The Wren*. "It would be a mammoth undertaking to form a corp of skilled women again. I don't know if I have the heart to become involved. Not without Constance. She was such a formidable commander."

"You have her daughter sleeping in the next room." Gerhardt refilled their empty glasses. "She seems to be a bright young thing. She saw through my disguise quick enough. She might well prove to be an asset to you in the coming days. She is fluent in three languages. I insisted she be educated to a high standard for a female of that class. That is not to be sniffed at, my dear."

"She is too young." Violet bit back a laugh. She had been younger than Krista when she'd presented herself to the first headquarters of the WRNS in Central Buildings Westminster. They hadn't even had a name then. But with older brothers and a father in the navy she had – like so many other young women – been desperate to do her bit. "She knows nothing of the world."

"You will have some time to train her up, I believe."

"Will you not take her with you? She is your niece after all."

"My dear Violet, there is a price on my head. A kill order – I will not serve Hitler in any way, shape or form. That child," he jerked his head in the direction of the bedroom, "has been at the very heart of espionage without ever knowing it. She must be protected until she can be educated in the ways of intrigue. She will not survive for long otherwise."

"Beaumont?" Violet had seen his reaction to that name. She knew the man slightly and had always thought him an insignificant little paper-pusher. She should have remembered that such a man made the best kind of spy.

"Not only Beaumont but the auberge itself is under suspicion." Gerhardt, as soon as they arrived at Mecelen had sought out a man who had been warning of the coming war for years. He had taken the time to pass along a message giving details of what had been discovered this day. He hoped it reached the right people but he had done all that he could.

"I am struggling to believe that Europe once more faces war." Violet wondered if she had the strength to don the mantle of power she had worn in the last war again. "Britain is not ready to face the might of the German army."

"Violet," Gerhardt gulped the last of the cognac in his glass, "if you had seen what I have seen. No one is ready to face the monster that is about to be unleashed on the world. The Russians are still saying they will fight from horseback for heaven's sake. The leaders of other nations think that talking about peace will help. Hitler will not be stopped in his march to power. We must all band together to stop him or the world will not be a place I want to live. *He must be stopped!*" He beat a clenched fist on the arm of his chair. "I need your contacts, Violet. You must introduce me to men

59

who will listen to reason. I have seen the factories churning out tanks. I have shivered in horror at the actions of young men of good family. My own sons wear brown shirts, for God's sake! I have failed to talk sense into their young heads. They march around shouting *Heil Hitler* with the rest of them. It is a nightmare. We two must convince the people who have the ears of those in power. Britain must begin to gather its forces or all will be lost."

Chapter 7

KRISTA WAS THE FIRST TO WAKE the next morning. She had a moment of terror as she tried to make sense of her surroundings. The room she was in was far more luxurious than her own little attic bedroom. She was underneath the bedclothes. How had that happened? There was a long well-stuffed bolster pillow running along one side of her body. She raised her head up slightly and almost gasped aloud at the sight of Miss Andrews sleeping on the other side of the bolster.

She slipped from the bed, trying not to wake the other woman. She dressed swiftly in the clothes she'd removed the previous night. She folded her borrowed nightdress and put it on top of the chest of drawers.

She took her handkerchief-wrapped money and letter from the top of the dresser and returned them to her skirt pockets.

In the sitting room she sought paper and something to write with. She found what she needed in a leather folder on top of one of the tables. In English she wrote that she had gone to seek something to eat and would return before they would miss her. She left the note lying on top of the folder and, with her heart thumping loudly, made her way out into the corridor in search of a bathroom.

She stifled a cry of delight when she saw a sign for a bathroom on one of the doors in the wide hallway. She was in dire need of the facilities. She locked the door at her back and swiftly took care of her bodily needs.

There was a well-stocked wicker basket of traveller's emergency supplies on the sink unit in the room. Krista had need of everything the basket contained but did not want to disturb the perfection of the arrangement with its bows and pretty rolls of towelling. She dropped to her knees and, with fingers mentally crossed that it was not locked, opened the cupboard doors underneath the unit. As she had thought – replacement supplies were kept close to hand. She took a toothbrush, a small tin of powdered toothpaste, a small square of soft sweet-smelling soap and a complimentary comb. She would take these items with her. She took one of the towelling facecloths from a stack and stood to take care of her needs.

She washed her body and restored order to her appearance. When she had done as much as she could she rolled the supplies she used and hid them at the very back of the unit. She would purchase a bag to carry her purloined goods in. With a skip in her steps she prepared to explore the world around her. She doubted the other two would be awake for hours yet. Perhaps it was stupid of her to risk being left behind in a strange town but she could not sit and wait for them to wake. There was a whole new world to explore – for her at least.

She ran down the wide staircase, not wanting to take the lift as they had the night before. She wanted to be out and about. She called a polite good morning to the night watchman who pulled open the door to the hotel at her approach. She stepped out into a wonderland. Dawn was only just bringing light to the sky but the world that opened before her was breathtakingly beautiful.

She walked out into the centre of the square and simply stood.

"Beautiful, is it not?" a voice said in Flemish.

Krista turned to find an old man, heavy broad-head sweeping brush in hand, smiling at her.

"Do you speak French?" she asked in French, mimicking Miss Andrews, a woman who spoke fluent French with the most dreadful British accent.

"But of course," the old man said. "Beautiful, is it not?" he said again in French.

"I have never seen anything like it."

The square was made up of tall old buildings overshadowed by an enormous cathedral. Each building was of a different shape and colour.

"You are standing in Grote Mart or Grand Market

if you prefer," the old man rested on his brush to say. "It is a mixture of sixteenth-century Renaissance and eighteenth-century Rococo." He smiled broadly, displaying a mouth with very few teeth but the laughter in his eyes was charming. "Or so I am told."

"What is that called?" Krista pointed to the cathedral.

"That is St. Rumbold's Cathedral," he told her with a proud expression. He stared at her for a moment before asking, "What is a young beauty such as you doing out and about all alone?"

"I am hungry and thirsty." Krista could see workers behind the glass of the restaurants on the ground floor of the many hotels. She dreaded to think how much it would cost to break her fast in one of those.

"You should not be walking the streets alone." The old man looked at her under beetling brows. "And it costs a small fortune to dine in one of those fancy places." A jerk of his head in the direction of one of the many restaurants accompanied his words. "Do you wish to spend a fortune?"

"I would prefer not to," Krista said with a smile.

"There is a café down that lane," he said, pointing. "It is not very far along it. Tell the waiter that old Claus sent you. He will look after you, and your coffee and croissant will not break the Bank of England." He chuckled.

"Thank you." Krista was grateful for the advice. She found the fancy restaurants intimidating. "I'll enjoy the view of the square before taking your advice." She began to walk away. "It was lovely speaking with you!" she called over her shoulder.

The old man returned to his sweeping, shaking his head over the youth of today.

"Miss, you asked to be notified when the King's suite ordered breakfast."

Krista had returned to the hotel clutching a small pale-blue hardboard case. It was cheap but she thought it looked beautiful with its dark-blue leather corners and handle. She'd found the case and other emergency supplies like knickers in the side street the old man had pointed out. A large warehouse holding the market stalls that would be set out around the square had been open. She'd entered and the stallholders had been more than willing to sell her their goods. She'd had coffee and a croissant before returning to the hotel. She'd put the items from the bathroom into the case and now felt like a world traveller as she waited for her travelling companions to wake.

"Thank you." She grabbed her new case and hurried along to join the others.

"Where have you been?" Gerhardt snapped as soon as he opened the suite door to Krista's knock. "It would serve you right if we had gone away and left you here."

"You worried us, Krista," Miss Andrews said from her place at the table. There was a generous spread of breakfast pastries on the table. The delicious smell of coffee permeated the suite. "Join us." She gestured towards the table.

"Thank you." Krista took a seat at the table. The position gave her a bird's-eye view over the square. "I'm sorry I worried you both but I couldn't sit still and wait for you to wake."

"What have you there?" Gerhardt pointed at the blue case.

"I bought myself a small case and some necessities." She helped herself to coffee while he returned to his seat. He was once more wearing what she thought of as his 'fat suit'. "I know from the auberge that people talk when you arrive somewhere without any luggage. I will need to seek work and a place to live when we reach our destination. I needed something of my own to take with me. I hope you don't mind?"

"We will be leaving as soon as we have broken our fast." He ignored her comments. "Violet, have you any suggestions as to what we can do with the papers this young woman brought to us?" He could use those orders to prove his points to the people he hoped to speak with in England. He didn't want to leave them behind if they could possibly take them with them safely.

"If I might make a suggestion?" Krista hastily swallowed the croissant slathered with jam that she had just bitten into.

"Speak!" Gerhardt snapped.

"Miss Andrews, that hat you were wearing yesterday …" she paused for a moment, "are you going to wear it again today?"

"Yes." Gerhardt was the one to answer. "I know you dislike it, Violet, but it gives you the appearance of a flibbertigibbet and distracts the eye from your clever face."

"It would appear I will be wearing the dratted thing," Violet sighed. "Why are you asking?"

"There is a rip in the lining of that hat." Krista continued to eat her second breakfast of the morning.

"I played with it many times." She wiped her lips with her napkin. "I bought a travelling sewing kit. We could put the papers into the crown of the hat and sew them inside. It's a simple matter."

"What a clever idea!" Violet looked into smiling blue eyes that looked so much like those of her dear friend Constance when she was up to mischief. "I can coil my hair and use many hatpins to keep the thing in place. What say you, Bertram?" It was important to keep up the subterfuge.

"Tend to that while we finish up here, Krista," Gerhardt said. "I want to be on the road to Antwerp as soon as possible. We should catch the second tide."

Krista picked up her case and left the table to seek out the hat.

"How shall we travel to England?" Violet leaned over the table to ask Gerhardt. "I have only my own papers on my person. I am presuming that we do not want to travel under our own names? Krista has no papers at all."

"I know many of the owners and captains of cargo vessels sailing out of Antwerp to Folkestone in England. I have used them to ship my wines. Then too I have the money to bribe one to look the other way as we board his vessel." He had thought long and hard about how he would escape when it became necessary. As he knew it would.

"Krista ..."

"Yes?" Krista appeared in the doorway of the bedroom.

"You need to remember to address us as 'Mother' and 'Father'." Gerhardt pushed back his chair. "It is vital you make no mistakes after we leave this room."

"Yes, Father," Krista almost blushed to address Herr Baron so familiarly but it was necessary. She could do this.

"I'm going to the bathroom." Violet desperately needed some time alone to gather her thoughts and prepare for the day ahead. "When you have finished with the hat, would you be so kind as to repack the items the maid removed from my suitcase, Krista?"

"Yes, Mother." Krista stepped back into the bedroom.

"Don't take too long, Violet." Gerhardt wanted to get on the road as soon as possible. He wanted to be in Antwerp long before second tide. He had matters to arrange.

Gerhardt stood in the middle of the sitting room of the suite, his eyes running over his two travelling companions. "Before I call a porter to remove our luggage, let us each examine the other. We must make sure we have everything we need with us. There will be no searching for last-minute items when we reach the docks. The car will be lifted onto the deck of the ship while we walk on. The wind on the water can freeze your bones so we must be well wrapped up – which is a blessing – much can be hidden under clothing."

"You need to remember to wear your gloves, Father." Krista was wearing a Burberry trench-coat belonging to the Baron. She felt very much the world traveller in the coat that had become famous by being the garment of choice for the commanders in WWI. The coat would be knee-length on a man but reached almost to Krista's shoes. Miss Andrews had placed a pretty silk scarf into the neck of the coat. She could pull that over her head when they were out in the fresh air.

"From this moment on I am Bertram Standish,' said Gerhardt. "Remember it. Bertram Standish, an Englishman travelling with his wife Ann and daughter Christine. It is vital we make no mistakes."

"Yes, Father."

"Certainly, Bertram."

"Ann, do you have enough hatpins in place to hold that hat onto your head even in gale-force winds?" he asked.

"The hat is practically cemented in place and I have a scarf to pull over it when we take to the sea," Violet pulled a silk headscarf from the pocket of her full-length mink coat.

"Then we appear to be ready to face the world. From the moment we leave this room we must be aware of everything going on around us, while giving the impression of travellers eager to reach their home port. It is imperative we reach England safely."

"What are your thoughts, Violet?" Gerhardt asked as they motored along towards Antwerp.

"We must head towards London." Violet had been giving a great deal of thought to the matter of help. "I think the best option for me is to travel to the headquarters of the Association of Wrens. There will be women there very much aware of what is going on in the world. It would be best if I visit for the first time alone. I can feel out the situation before asking for advice. What do you think?"

"I have friends of many years in London." Gerhardt too had been planning the best way to approach his uneasy situation. He would be seen as a traitor to his country. Nothing could be further from the truth. He loved his country. Had always been proud of being German. Now he felt lost, cast adrift with no clear idea of his final destination.

He checked the roads around him carefully. They were busy here as they approached the port of Antwerp. "I will take a room at my London club."

Krista listened to them, wondering what would happen to her when they reached England. She had never been far from the Auberge du Village in Metz. What was to become of her? She remained silent, waiting to see what the day would bring. Whatever it was, it was better than anything the Dumas family and Maurice La Flandre had planned for her.

Chapter 8

KRISTA WAS AFRAID TO BLINK HER EYES, afraid she might miss something. She could spend weeks here enjoying this unfamiliar landscape. So many people, such hustle and bustle. How was anything achieved in the chaos she was watching? She was barely aware of the man ushering them towards the first-class waiting room set behind a waist-high barrier on the dock of Antwerp.

There were so many ships tied up at the docks. Where did they all sail to? How wonderful it would be to be a sailor and choose to sail the world's oceans! How would it feel to wake up knowing you were travelling to a far-flung destination in a strange world new to you? The very thought of such adventure stole her breath.

She refused to enter the waiting room with her

travelling companions. She couldn't bear to be locked away from the wonderful sights, sounds and smells around her. She stood on the walkway behind the barrier, her eyes almost burning as she tried to take in all there was to see.

She watched families clutching what appeared to be their worldly belongings being herded into a barnlike building further down the dock. The people seemed uniformly dressed in dark clothing, with worry etched into the parents' grey faces. Those people were not travelling for pleasure.

She held her breath as a horse in an open wooden box that looked somewhat like a stable stall was lifted into the air from the dockside and slowly moved through the air towards a nearby ship. The poor animal. She wouldn't like to be lifted in such a fashion. The apparatus holding it in the air looked like a giant slingshot to her eyes. Would the car be lifted in such a fashion? She followed the animal's flight with her heart in her mouth. There were men on the deck of the ship, obviously waiting to take delivery of the animal. They had best be careful. If she had been forced to travel in such a fashion, she would exit that box with her fists clenched ready to fight. That horse had deadly hooves to kick out with. She released the breath she had not been aware of holding when the animal landed safely on the deck of the ship.

Her attention was drawn to a man who strode the docks like a colossus. He stood head and shoulders over every other man around him. His shoulders in the navy double-breasted jacket he wore seemed to fill her vision. He had a peaked hat pulled down over an explosion of red hair and his beard was thick and full. He was stopped frequently by men clutching papers while she watched fascinated.

She narrowed her eyes and stared at one of the men following in the footsteps of the colossus. Did he look familiar? Where had she seen him before?

"Christine, what on earth are you doing standing out here?"

Money changed hands as Gerhardt tipped the man who had carried their hand luggage and shown them to the waiting room. "There is a fire in the waiting room. Go inside. You'll catch your death standing out here." Gerhardt ignored their guide who walked away whistling, pushing the generous tip into his trouser pocket.

"Father, I am fine. I couldn't sit down and wait if you forced me." Krista felt weak at the knees. She had just remembered where she had seen the man on the dock who had attracted her attention. "There is so much to see."

"You will have a better view from the deck of our ship." Gerhardt wanted to mop his brow. He was nervous. They were so close to escape. He wanted to be on board ship and sailing away from this place. He would not feel safe even when he set foot on British soil but he'd feel a damn sight safer with the sea between him and those who sought him.

"That man –" Krista pointed.

"It is rude to point, child." Gerhardt put his gloved hand over hers and lowered the pointing finger.

"Sorry, Father, but does that man not look like the drawings of Sinbad the Sailor?" She was careful to remain in character. She had been warned that their every word and movement could be under scrutiny. She put her arm through Gerhardt's, feeling daring – but surely a fond daughter would do something similar? She had no experience to draw upon.

Gerhardt stiffened at her unexpected familiarity. "That is the harbour master. A fine man."

"The man following behind him . . ." Krista almost buried her head in his chest as she spoke softly. "The one wearing the dark-brown suit with the light-brown shirt." She waited until he looked down at her. "I believe I have seen him many times before – he has been a guest at the Auberge du Village ... in the company of Monsieur Beaumont."

Gerhardt put his arm around her shoulder and led her into the waiting room. They were too exposed outside, in plain view of anyone on the dock who cared to look in their direction. He stepped further into the room before releasing Krista and turning to look out the window. He stared at the man Krista had pointed out.

"Are you sure?" he asked.

"What is going on?" Violet hated to leave the warmth of the fire but she needed to know. She walked over to stand beside them.

"That man in the brown suit snapping on the heels of that tall man, the harbour master," Krista said softly, "has visited the auberge many times in the last year. He and Monsieur Beaumont dine together frequently when he visits."

"Do you know him, Bertram?" Violet squinted to bring the man more clearly into view.

"I do not." Gerhardt had no memory of the man.

"Daring of him to state his affiliations so openly." The brown shirts of the Nazi youth had become infamous. The man's clothing was almost a perfect match for their uniform.

"It gives those of us he hunts warning." Gerhardt continued to take note of everything about the man.

"He cannot be allowed to see us." Violet shivered. "If he has indeed been a frequent visitor to the Auberge du Village in Metz he will know Krista by sight. And he may well have seen me in the village. I have a certain reputation as the eccentric Englishwoman."

The three stood in the shadows, watching the man as he sought the harbour master's attention. They could do nothing but wait to see what would happen. Any sudden action on their part would draw too much attention to them.

A rap of knuckles on the waiting-room door had each of them stiffening. The knock was followed by the door opening and a smiling weather-beaten face appearing in the opening.

"Mr and Mrs Standish?" the man enquired.

"I am Standish." Gerhardt almost pulled his shoulders back but a sharp tap on his back from Krista stopped him. Her movement was hidden from the man in the doorway.

"Jim, the captain, thought you and your family might like a pot of tea or something while you wait. Shan't be long now until we have all the cargo loaded and you can come aboard. Sorry for the delay." He gave a gap-toothed grin.

"An Englishman by heaven!" Violet, the only true English person of their little group, stepped forward. Her companions might be able to fool foreigners into believing they were English, but she doubted an Englishman would be deceived for very long. "Come in and close the door. You are letting the warm air out!" She waved towards the fireplace. "Bertram, Christine, go sit by the fire. The pair of you must be frozen after standing outside for so long."

"There is a lazy wind blowing out there right enough." Jim stepped into the room, closing the door at his back.

"I beg your pardon?" Violet raised an eyebrow at the cheeky chap.

"That's what me mother calls it," he grinned. "A wind that's too lazy to go around you but goes through you!"

"It is brisk out there," Gerhardt dared to say. He couldn't remain silent and let the woman do all the talking. It would not be in character for the man he was trying to portray.

"Now, how about that pot of tea?" Jim had things to do but the captain wanted to be sure this posh couple had nothing to complain to the shipping company about. He'd ordered Jim to see to their needs.

"A pot of tea would be wonderful. We have been travelling for months. We," she gestured to the others, "have been drinking coffee! I must admit a proper cup of tea is one of the many things I miss about home."

"Well, to be honest, ma'am," Jim shrugged, "if I were you, I'd wait until I got home before having tea.

It's a fright here. You'd be safer staying with the coffee."

"Ah well, when in Rome!" Violet laughed. "We thank you for the offer but we will take your advice and wait until we reach England's shores before we drink tea. We are not in need of anything at the moment."

"Right you are, ma'am." Jim pulled his forelock and with a smile stepped out of the room.

"Watch him, Violet." Gerhardt didn't leave his chair, his voice almost a whisper.

"It would appear that the man in the brown suit is interested in who we are." Violet was careful to keep out of sight of the people on the dock. She watched as the brown-suited man stopped the English sailor. Money changed hands as she watched. "He is not a very skilled spy if that is indeed what he is. He actually pointed towards this waiting room if you can believe that." She continued to watch what was happening on the dock.

Gerhardt wanted to move. He needed to get out of this small room. "That man strutting around the dock is one of the many bully boys trying to make themselves important in the new regime. Do not underestimate him and his ilk."

"He is once more running after the harbour master." Violet turned to look at her companions. "Judging from the body language, he does not appear to be popular with the men working the docks. He is receiving some very pointed glares."

"You always were good at judging the mood of a crowd," Gerhardt said as he stood up.

"Father!" Krista snapped before he could take a

step. "You simply must remember to slouch. Look at your posture!" She waved a hand in his direction, feeling very daring. But if the man didn't take the steel out of his backbone he was going to give them all away to anyone caring to look. "You look all set to bang your heels together. That is a very German habit, one you must repress. You do not look anything like an overweight bumbling Englishman at the moment." She waited tensely to see if the man glaring at her would box her ears. But it needed to be said. She had no wish to be discovered trying to flee the country with a wanted man.

"The child is right." Violet didn't have to look to understand what Krista saw. "You must strive to stay in character, Bertram."

"You are both correct." Gerhardt sat down again with a sigh. "This waiting when we are so close to escape is wearing on the nerves. It has been a very long time since I needed to hide who and what I am."

Chapter 9

"CHRISTINE," VIOLET TURNED FROM THE window, "please keep watch." She gestured for Krista to stand up from her chair close to the fire. "Tell us if anything seems noteworthy to you." She almost collapsed into the chair. It had been many years since she'd had to be constantly on her guard. She didn't know if she could do it all again. She had been a young woman during the last war. Was she too old to become involved in the one everyone seemed to think was coming? But surely to goodness saner heads would prevail and stop the carnage that war brought? She wanted to drop her head into her hands and weep. But she straightened her spine. She had never been a weak woman.

"Bertram," she leaned forward to ask, "who is that British car registered to?"

That officious little man in brown looked like a pencil-pusher to her. He'd have his nose into everyone else's business if she was any judge. Such men had been the bane of her existence in the last war.

"Bertram Standish." The man assuming that name leaned his head closer to Violet's. "He is a grand chap. At this moment in time he is in Berlin preparing for the upcoming air show. I offered to drive his car back to England. He plans to buy a plane if he finds one that pleases him. I expect he will fly his new plane home or hitch a ride home with one of the English pilots taking part in the show."

"The world has gone mad." Violet wanted to punch something. Imagine, travelling to an air show in the very heart of that madman's nest. She wondered what would happen to all of the artists and musicians visiting Germany. Did no one see the storm clouds gathering over Europe? "Air-shows – invitations to the European upper-level social set, to visit and party with that man. Have you seen the photographs in the newspapers? The list of people flocking to his side? Have they all run mad?" She leaned her head back, fighting tears. "Or are we being alarmist, my dear?"

Krista watched the crowds of people being escorted onto the ships waiting on the docks. The man in the brown suit appeared to be paying a great deal of attention to the shivering crowd but he wasn't doing anything to stop their leaving as far as she could see.

Gerhardt too was heartsick. "People don't want to believe that the men in power would be insane enough to force us into another war. But I have seen too much on my journeys to promote the family business. I couldn't close my eyes to what is going on – and, to be honest with you, I am terrified by what I have seen. No one, no country is ready for what that man Hitler has planned."

"I am as guilty as the next man of closing my eyes to what is happening around me." Violet had been desperately hoping that saner heads would prevail.

"I thought you were going to shoot me when I insisted you accompany me on this trip." Gerhardt knew he'd been taking his life in his hands when he'd appealed to Violet for help. He'd had no choice in the matter. The German forces were searching for a man alone. He had hoped an Englishman travelling with a wife would escape detection. Krista, in the role of his daughter, was an added bonus to his disguise.

"I had made a nice little life for myself," Violet said.

"You were never meant for a life of bucolic bliss, my dear Ann." Gerhardt had never understood how a woman who had been instrumental in saving lives and organising a force as powerful as the WRNS in the war had ever been able to settle to a life teaching little snot-nosed children to speak and read English. "Why did you never marry?" She was a good-looking woman. It wouldn't have been for lack of opportunity.

Violet stared across the fire at the man daring to ask her such a personal question. She bit her lip against the fiery words that wanted to escape her. How dare he? He was probably waiting for her to give him a sob story about the love of her life lost in the trenches. It was a familiar story after all. There were a great many women enjoying the pity of their friends as they told their sob stories, over and over again.

"The institution of marriage never appealed to me," she contented herself with saying. Now was not the time to get into discussion about the horror she'd witnessed in the life of her own friends – intelligent women who had given up everything to marry the man of their dreams. Not for her the role of the little woman supporting her big strong man. She had spent years in the Wrens doing the work while some man reaped the rewards and honours. She had a small inheritance that allowed her to live quietly while answering to no man. The life she had made for herself suited her. She preferred not to think about what might become of her now.

Krista was not paying attention to the conversation going on behind her. She was looking out the window as ordered but not really seeing what was in front of her. She was worried. What was to become of her? She was unaware of lifting her hands and rubbing at her temples. Her head hurt. She had been speaking English almost constantly since she left the auberge. Her brain felt as if it were leaking out of her ears.

Would she be able to make herself understood in England? Would she understand what was said to her? She hadn't understood a word that English sailor said to Miss Andrews in spite of spending years studying with the help of the British Broadcasting Corporation tapes that Miss Andrews insisted her students mimic.

Her attention was diverted to a scuffle taking place amongst the people trying to board one of the ships. She narrowed her eyes, trying to see clearly what was taking place.

"I believe you need to see what is going on outside," she half-turned to say to her travelling companions.

"What's happening?" Violet was glad to get away from Gerhardt and his questioning. Her life was none of his business.

"I don't know but come look." Krista put her hands in her pockets, trying not to point.

"Where?" Violet put her hand on Krista's shoulder and followed the direction the girl indicated with a jerk of her head.

"*Gerhardt!*" Violet gasped, forgetting to call him Bertram, unable to believe what she was seeing.

He joined the two women at the window.

"We can't all stand here like shop-front dummies," he said but then froze as he registered the scene on the docks.

"Those are not Belgian soldiers." Violet watched in disbelief as soldiers forcibly dragged men out of the crowd of passengers standing on the dock.

"No," Gerhardt sighed. "They are German." He watched as one man was pushed to the ground and kicked when he tried to object to being dragged away from his family. He had seen scenes like this in his own country. He'd been able to intervene. In Germany he was a titled gentleman with something of a reputation. Here, he was an obese, pompous Englishman. What could he do?

"How in the name of goodness are they getting away with this?" Violet winced at the rough treatment being handed out to the passengers. No one was objecting, not even the Belgian policemen accompanying the German troops. The sailors on the docks were pointedly not seeing what was going on in front of them.

"I am not surprised to see German troops here. Our countries share a coastline. The Flemish people in this part of Belgium are proud of their German heritage." Gerhardt lowered his eyes to his feet, ashamed of the actions of his countrymen. He wanted to shoot them down like the dogs they were. But what use would that be? He could not win this fight. He was not afraid to die but he refused to offer up his life until he had made powerful men listen to him. He had to try. That man Hitler must be stopped.

"The amount of money being spent bribing officials to look away must be enormous." Violet put one hand in front of her mouth. She wanted to run out there and start laying waste to those soldiers – men who thought they were above everyone else.

"Hitler has become very wealthy," Gerhardt said. "He has been systematically stripping wealthy Jews of their belongings. He has taken many, many millions of deutschmarks from the heads of families. He is a thief offering 'your money or your life' – that is what the old highwaymen used to say, is it not?" He knew wealthy German Jews were being encouraged to leave the country. Joseph Goebbels had recently sent out a memo encouraging Hitler to put a system of publicly marking Jews in place.

The three stood silently watching. They watched as the men were shoved up against a nearby warehouse. The German officer separated from the group and began taking slow deliberate steps along the line of cowering men.

"That man appears to be enjoying his moment of

power a tad too much."

The officer had backhanded a young man who apparently had the nerve to question his actions. An older man grabbed at the younger before he could collapse to the ground. He received a punch to his stomach for his daring.

"We cannot sit here like rats in a trap, waiting for that bully to grab us." Violet looked around the little room, frantically searching for something that could be used as a weapon. They had left their guns hidden in the car. Stupid.

Gerhardt pulled the two women from the window by their elbows. "Listen to me closely now. *Neither of you speak German.*" He shook them by their elbows. "*Do you understand?*" He shook them. "*Not one word of German, do you understand?*"

The two women never took their eyes from his face as they nodded.

"From what we have observed," Gerhardt took a deep breath before continuing, "they appear to only be interested in males. You two must leave me here – make your way to the ship. The *Swallow* is berthed on the fourth dock to your left as you exit this room. The captain is a good man. Vickers will see you both right if I should fail to join you."

"I believed my worth to you was as a shield you could hide behind?" Violet regretted bringing Krista with them. "Those men," she pointed in the direction of the window and the German soldiers, "look like they would shoot first and ask questions later."

Krista didn't know what to do or what to say. This situation was far outside her experience.

"Plans change at a moment's notice and we must be ready to change with them," Gerhardt said. He was keeping an eye on the activity outdoors. He did not want the women here when those soldiers reached this room – as he was sure they would. "We have no papers for Krista and my own are forged. I cannot allow you two to be placed in danger on my behalf. Those men will have no mercy for anyone discovered with me. I cannot worry about your safety while fighting for my own freedom."

"Fighting!" Violet gasped, thinking of the weapons the German soldiers carried openly.

"It may not come to that." Gerhardt would do everything in his power to walk away from this room. But he would not be responsible for harm coming to two innocent women because of him. "I need you both to be brave. You must walk out of this room with your heads held high and disdain for all who try to stop you." He smiled sadly. "I have seen you stare disdainfully enough times, my dear Ann. It is very off-putting, I do assure you."

They stood for a moment, each unsure of what to say. The situation was unspeakable.

"Come." Gerhardt turned the women around to face the doorway. "We have no time to waste."

"I don't like leaving you like this," Violet objected.

But Krista wanted to pick up her skirts and run to the safety of the ship. She had no desire to face heavily armed German soldiers.

"I know, my dear, but needs must. You two must leave me here for your own safety. I never intended to put you in danger. Go now."

He waited while they each picked up their bags before almost pushing them towards the door of the waiting room.

"I will sit here and smoke my last cigar and wait for developments," he said.

He shrugged when Violet glared at him over her shoulder.

"Cigars are a filthy habit, Bertram, as I have told you many times before." She was fighting tears. She could do nothing to help him in this situation – and he was right – his worry over them could endanger him. She would have to get Krista away and pray to a God that she had almost forgotten that Gerhardt could talk himself out of this situation.

"God go with you, my dears." He opened the door to allow them to step outside. "I will join you if and when I can."

He stood in the open doorway, watching them walk across the quayside. He closed the door with a sigh when it appeared that their appearance attracted no attention.

He sat in the chair to one side of the fire and took out the last of his expensive cigars. Pulling a silver tool from his trousers pocket, he stared at it.

"It is the little things that trap you," he muttered, staring at the silver cigar cutter. The tool bore his family crest and initials. "Stupid." He longed to throw the item from him, but it was an expensive article and would attract attention if found. "Time to gird my loins and enter battle."

He cut the end from the cigar then bent to shove the cutter into his half-boots.

87

He puffed smoke into the room and waited. He looked around him at the room, which appeared dingy to his eyes. "I never thought I would meet my end in a waiting room." He grinned wryly. "Mother always did say I'd come to a bad end."

Chapter 10

"ARE WE REALLY TO LEAVE HIM ALONE?" Krista felt an itch between her shoulder blades. She longed to turn her head to see what was happening behind her. She kept her eyes focused on the busy docks, avoiding the men working to load the many ships. The noise and bustle was almost frightening to someone unused to such frantic activity.

"What do you suggest we do?" Violet wanted to scream her frustration to the sky. She hadn't wanted to come on this journey. She'd been content in her little cottage.

"I don't know." Surely they could do something? It felt wrong to turn her back on a man she had known all of her life – but how did one go about facing down men with guns?

"Nor do I." Violet lowered her eyelids and allowed her eyes to search the area around them. They were attracting no special attention as far as she could see. "Keep your chin up, shoulders back and head towards the ship as we were ordered. We cannot afford to attract attention."

"What if they are not ready for us to board the ship?" Krista fretted.

"If they can board horses and grain, they can bloody well board humans!" Violet snapped.

They walked briskly along the dock, looking for the ship that would carry them to England.

The man calling himself Bertram Standish sat waiting, listening intently to the noise from outside, praying the women would escape detection. He gave every appearance of a man at ease, in spite of his heart thundering so hard it almost rattled his chest. He used his heels to push his chair farther from the fire. He could not afford to appear to sweat. It wouldn't be long now.

Even though he had been expecting it, the slamming open of the waiting-room door and the noise it made as it bounced against the wall almost caused him to jump.

"That, gentlemen, is no way to enter a room," Gerhardt snapped in English. He put his cigar in his mouth, glaring at the three German soldiers standing in the doorway. "And, either come in or go out – you are letting the cold in." He leaned back in his chair, continuing to puff on his cigar.

"Your papers," the officer demanded.

"I am a British citizen – why on earth should I present my papers to you?"

He watched their fingers twitching on their weapons. They were not accustomed to people defying them. They considered themselves the elite.

"If you insist on staying, shut the door – this room is becoming chilly." Gerhardt watched closely. He noticed that the two young soldiers standing at the officer's back twitched but didn't react in any other way. "What is this all about? You have been making a nuisance of yourself on the docks, I noticed."

Gerhardt listened as the officer ordered his two soldiers to return to the dock – he assured his men that the fat Englishman posed no threat to one such as he. He would check his papers and rejoin them soon in their search.

The officer slammed the door after the retreating soldiers.

He stood for a moment and took a deep breath – before snapping his fingers at Gerhardt. "Your papers – *now!*" He returned his gun to its case on his hip.

Gerhardt reached into the chest pocket of his jacket and withdrew his English passport. With his eyes locked on the other man's, he held out the document.

There was silence while the officer examined the passport.

"Excellent forgery." He slammed the document into Gerhardt's outstretched hand.

Gerhardt continued to study the other man.

"You are a traitor!" the officer spat.

"So I would appear to one such as you."

"You were ordered to present yourself to your old

unit." The officer turned and stared out the window, watching his men search the docks. The Führer had issued a list of scientists and men of wealth to be detained if seen.

"I never received those orders," Gerhardt replied.

"Because you made sure you would not be there to receive them."

"What are you going to do, Heinrich?"

"You will address me as Hauptsturmführer Wessel."

"Hauptsturmführer already? I was not aware of your attending officer training, Heinrich."

"You do not know everything I do." Heinrich Wessel put both hands behind his back and stalked about the room, chin held high.

"You look ridiculous posturing like that, Heinrich."

He swung around. "You dare!" A hand unbuttoned the case holding the gun at his hip.

"If you are going to shoot me, Heinrich, may I request that you wait until I have finished my cigar?" Gerhardt puffed languidly.

"I should shoot you down like the dog you are." Heinrich's face turned red, the veins in his neck noticeably throbbing. Why had he been the one to find this man?

"You could do that, of course, but think of the effect your actions will have on you and your career. Not to mention how your beloved older sister will be disgraced."

"My sister is a saint, above reproach."

"Will your Führer think that way?"

Heinrich Wessel continued to caress the leather cover on his hip holster. He wanted to shoot this man and walk away with his head high.

"You need to make up your mind quickly." Gerhardt drew his gold pocket watch from his waistcoat and made a production of consulting it, despite the overlarge station clock that hung on a nearby wall. "I do not want to miss my ship."

He waited to see what the other man would do.

"You can shoot me and drag my carcass out of this room, loudly shouting your victory," Gerhardt said softly, his eyes on his watch. "Should you do that, you may perhaps be lauded for your actions. However, in no time you will find yourself slipping down the ranks. After all, you are related to a traitor."

"We share no blood."

"You and your kind are hunting men and women who have the blood of a Jew from generations back. I am sure if someone interested searched hard enough, they would find some vague blood connection between us. We are both after all members of the German upper class."

Gerhardt watched his wife's younger brother sweat and caress the weapon at his hip. Was it any wonder that he'd been unable to talk sense into his sons' heads? It was clear to him now that their beloved Uncle Heinrich had been filling their heads with rubbish about the power and beauty of the German Reich.

"Should you shoot me and declare me a traitor, my wife – your sister – will lose the status that is so important to her. My sons will lose their heritage. You will be closely related to men others will spit on. *Make up your mind, Heinrich*. It is time to fish or cut bait." Gerhardt wanted to box the young man's ears. While he had been working all the hours God made to support his people and his estate this man had been enjoying the rewards of those labours. How dare he stand before him now and judge him!

"There may be some among my men who recognise you."

"I have no time for this." Gerhardt stood and began to don his outdoor wear. He pulled his collar up around his neck before wrapping his white scarf twice around it. He put his hat on his head and, with a glare for a man he had watched grow from a boy, he picked up his hand luggage and began to walk out of the room. If Heinrich was going to shoot him, he could shoot him in the back.

"I will not wish you well," Heinrich spat.

"I would not expect it." Gerhardt wondered what would happen to his family in the coming days. He could not stay as head of the family. He would not serve in the German forces. It would be every man for himself from this moment on – he had done all he could to protect his family and estates.

While Gerhardt fought for his freedom Violet and Krista approached the ship. They didn't hesitate in climbing the wooden gangplank, holding their breath as it wobbled under their combined weight. Gripping each other tightly, they almost ran up the boards.

"What is going on? Where is Standish?" Captain William Vickers stood with his legs braced apart, staring at the two women. He had been in a sweat ever since he'd seen those German soldiers grabbing at male passengers. He was well acquainted with the man calling himself Standish. He had given his word to carry these two women safely to England if anything should happen to him. He prayed to God he wouldn't have to carry out his part of that agreement.

"Captain Vickers," Violet stared at the man blocking her way, "permission to come aboard?"

Vickers stepped back at the order couched as a request.

"Where is Standish?" He couldn't delay his sailing. The pilot boats that would lead him out were on a tight schedule. He needed to catch the tide.

"My husband insisted on enjoying one last cigar before sailing." Violet had to force herself not to look over her shoulder. "Filthy habit, as I tell him often." She shrugged and gave the frowning captain a bright smile. "The poor love is a terrible sailor. He wanted to relax for a moment before being subjected to a bout of *mal de mer*, don't you know? My daughter and I came on ahead as I cannot bear the smell of those fusty cigars and poor Christine is a martyr to her lungs – cannot stop coughing when her father lights up one of those dreadful things."

"I hope he won't be long." Captain Vickers felt his heart sink. "I have matters to attend to before sailing. If you will excuse me."

"I'll take you to your cabin, ladies." A sailor had appeared at Violet's elbow.

"Thank you." Violet took Krista's arm and towed her along after the sailor. They could do nothing to help and their presence on deck might well hinder Gerhardt in his efforts to escape.

Captain Vickers put the two women out of his mind. He stood watching the waiting-room door with his heart in his mouth. He waited for the appearance of a man he had called friend for many years. The cool wind blew the sweat from his brow, helping to hide his nerves. He avoided looking up at the crow's nest where he had a man in position ready to act at his signal, should the worse come to worst.

The door of the waiting room opened and his friend stepped out, closely followed by a German officer. He held his breath and nerve, waiting to see what would happen. The German officer remained standing in the open doorway of the waiting room, while the older man almost shuffled towards the waiting ship.

Vickers held his breath. Would he make it?

"*Halt!*" Heinrich shouted from the open doorway. He could not allow this man to escape. He must be returned to Germany to serve the Führer. The problem would then be out of his hands.

The shouted order in German rang across the dock. It attracted the attention of the German soldiers but was ignored by Gerhardt who increased his speed.

Vickers signalled with an arm.

A shot rang out.

The cement of the doorstop at the German officer's feet exploded in a shower of debris. There were startled shouts and the sound of heavy boots hitting the cobbled surface of the dock.

"*Signal the pilots! Prepare to set sail!*" Vickers shouted the order as he watched the activity on the dock.

Gerhardt lowered his body as he ran, wanting to present a smaller target. He moved with speed towards the ship in a crouched position.

He ran up the gangplank and Vickers and a sailor hauled him aboard. Vickers pushed him off his feet and against the side of the ship, hiding his presence from view of the docks. The sailor pulled the gangplank aboard.

"*Stay down, man!*" Vickers barked when the figure at his feet started to move. He waited a moment to be sure his order was being obeyed. "I haven't seen a trench trot like that in years." Men of WWI had learned to move at speed around the trenches while keeping their heads down.

"Amazing what comes back to you when you're in danger." Gerhardt was trying not to shake. "Who the hell took that shot?"

"Young seaman of mine. Has medals and trophies for marksmanship." Vickers continued to watch the frantic activity on dock. The stupid officer was still standing framed by the open doorway. Didn't the man know he was making a very attractive target of himself? Ah, well, if what he had been hearing from people in the know was true, the fool would learn or perish – as they had all had to in the last war.

The ship shuddered under his feet. They were about to slowly make their way out to sea.

"May I get up now?" Gerhardt almost wept in relief as he felt the engines of the ship take hold.

"*No, you bloody can't!*" Vickers was tempted to kick the man stretched out on his deck. How dare he ask him to shoot to kill if it looked like he was being taken into custody? He doubted the young man crouching up in the crow's nest had ever shot at a human being. Would he have been able to carry out the order? Thank God they didn't have to find out. Not today anyway.

"I am sorry for the position I put you in, my old friend."

Gerhardt lay on his back, looking up at the figure standing over him. "Trust me, it was necessary." He had never intended to be taken alive. He had seen what the new German Reich did to their prisoners – it was inhumane. It had been his good fortune that an old soldier like Vickers was captain of his getaway ship. A man who would be able to do what needed to be done. He needed to find someplace he could hide before reaction set in. Vickers would understand that.

In their cabin the two women felt the engines take hold. They looked at each other but didn't speak. What could they say?

They held their breath, wondering if the man who had led them this far had made it.

Violet walked to the window which gave a view out over the grey ocean. She was going home. What would she find there?

Krista took a seat in one of the soft chairs bolted to the deck. She was shaking and hoped her companion would not notice. Had the Baron managed to escape capture? When would they know? She was trying to focus on the answer to this question in order not to think about her own fate. She was sailing into the unknown. What would become of her?

To Be Continued . . .

Printed in Great Britain
by Amazon

51925174R00061